A Random House PICTUREBACK® Book

Thomas's ABC Book

Based on *The Railway Series* by the Rev. W. Awdry

Photographs by Kenny McArthur, David Mitton, and
Terry Permane for Britt Allcroft's production of
Thomas the Tank Engine and Friends

Thomas the Tank Engine & Friends A BRITT ALLCROFT COMPANY PRODUCTION Based on The Railway Series by
the Rev W Awdry. Copyright © Gullane (Thomas) LLC 1998. Photographs © Gullane (Thomas) Limited 1985, 1986. All rights
reserved under International and Pan-American Copyright Conventions. Published in the United States by Random House, Inc.,
New York, and simultaneously in Canada by Random House of Canada Limited, Toronto.

www.randomhouse.com/kids   www.thomasthetankengine.com

Library of Congress Cataloging-in-Publication Data

Thomas's ABC book / photographs by Kenny McArthur, David Mitton, and Terry Permane for Britt Allcroft's
production of Thomas the tank engine and friends. p. cm. "Based on the Railway series by the Rev. W. Awdry."
SUMMARY: An alphabet book featuring Thomas the tank engine and his friends.
ISBN 0-679-89357-1 (pbk.)
[1. Railroads—Trains—Fiction. 2. Alphabet.] I. McArthur, Kenny, ill. II. Mitton, David, ill. III. Permane, Terry, ill.
IV. Awdry, W. Railway series. V. Thomas the tank engine and friends. PZ7.T36965 1998 98-6233

Printed in the United States of America   July 1998   30 29 28 27 26 25 24 23 22

PICTUREBACK, RANDOM HOUSE and colophon, and PLEASE READ TO ME and colophon
are registered trademarks of Random House, Inc.

A is for all aboard.

"All aboard!" calls Thomas the Tank Engine.

B is for Bertie the Bus.

Bertie is Thomas's friend. *Beep! Beep!*

C is for coaches.

Annie and Clarabel are Thomas's coaches.

D is for Diesel.

Doesn't Diesel look grumpy today?

E is for Edward.

Edward, a kind engine, helps everyone.

F is for freight cars.

"Trick-trock!" say the silly freight cars.

G is for Gordon.

Gordon is a big, strong engine. *Poop! Poop!*

H is for Henry.

Here comes Henry under the bridge.

I is for important.

Trains do important work.

J is for James.

James is going on an exciting journey.

K is for kind. **L** is for little.

Kind little Edward is careful with freight cars.
Wheesh!

M is for men.

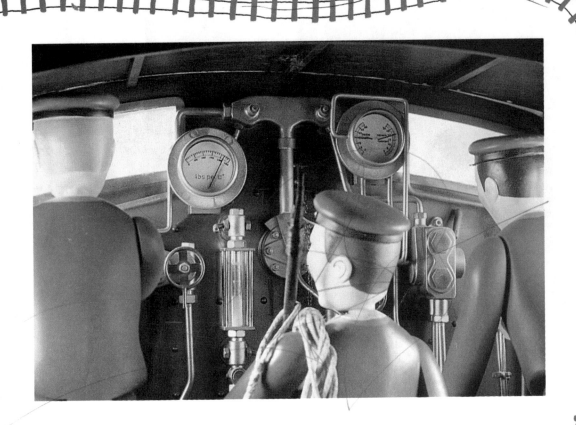

The men who drive the engine stand inside the cab.

N is for new.

Here's Henry with a new coat of paint.

O is for old-fashioned.

Toby the Tram Engine is old-fashioned but very helpful.

P is for Percy.

Percy is the little green engine. *Peep! Peep!*

Q is for quick.

James the Red Engine comes to a quick stop.

R is for rest.

Thomas and Percy rest in the railway station.

S is for Sir Topham Hatt.

Sir Topham Hatt runs the railroad.

T is for tracks.

Terence tells Thomas about his tracks.

U is for up.

Up on the bridge, Thomas chugs along happily.

V is for valley.

Thomas climbs out of the valley up the steep hill.

W is for whoosh! **X** is for eXpress.

Whoosh! Gordon the Big Engine pulls
the express.

Y is for yard. **Z** is for zip.

Zip! Zip! Thomas is busy in the yard—pushing and pulling. Isn't he a Really Useful Engine?